T. D. Ashcraft

BUMP &the GAME of

HIDE & SEEK

a Jump Splash book

Bump & the Game of Hide & Seek

Printed in the United States of America.

First Printing, 2020.

ISBN-13: 978-1-7327024-2-4

Jump Splash Publishing

Jump Splash
B O O K S
www.JumpSplashBooks.com

Dedicated with love . . .

To my beautiful wife and children.

To all of my nieces and nephews. (Welcome to the world, Olivia!)

To all of Bump's fans that have waited so patiently for this adventure.

And to the memory of Uncle Jeff. You were a source of encouragement from the very beginning and we love and miss you more than we can express.

Special thanks to Tonia Zara for naming our newest monster friend.

Bump has brought a brand-new friend
to play with in my room.

I think I see him over there,
disguised like he's a broom.

Bump says, "His name is Shifty.
He loves playing hide and seek.

But watch him on your turn to hide.
Sometimes he tends to peek."

Bump chooses to be seeker first
and then he turns around.

I rush to find a hiding place
without making a sound.

Bump quietly says, "Ready or not," after counting to 24.

I found a good place just in time, behind my closet door.

Bump quickly finds all our friends,
except for Shifty and me.

I move a bit behind the door
and gently hit my knee.

The sound gets Bump's attention.
He quickly turns around.

My noise has given me away.
I'm the next one to be found.

Shifty has just won the round,
so he is the next seeker.

We blindfold him while we all hide
'cause we know he is a peeker.

He's not a real great seeker
so it takes him quite a while.

I'm the last one found. "I win!"
I cheer and flash a great big smile.

My turn as seeker has finally come!
I cover up my eyes.

I start to count 1, 2, and 3
and then to my surprise...

I hear a crash so big and loud
it wakes my mom and dad.

I climb in bed and start to cry;
afraid they will be mad.

They rush right in and hug me tight.
They are not mad at all!

They thought I had a scary dream
or perhaps a nasty fall.

They tuck me back into my bed
and then turn off the light.

We'll pick up where we left our game
again another night.

About the Author

T.D. Ashcraft created his fun-loving title character, Bump, in 2008. Inspired by some of his favorite childhood authors—like Dr. Seuss and Mike Higgs—Ashcraft began writing Bump's series of adventures.

Ashcraft's stories are written to appeal to both children and parents alike. The characters are colorful, creative, and fun and each adventure teaches an important lesson while maintaining a rhyming pattern that's easy to read.

Joining the Jump Splash Books family in 2017, Ashcraft has continued working on more adventures for Bump as well as partnering on other projects. (Stay tuned!)

Ashcraft lives in Columbus, OH with his wife, their two kids, and their puppy.

Look for new projects from T.D. Ashcraft and Jump Splash Books coming soon!

Adding a
SPLASH
of Imagination

Jump Splash
B O O K S

THE TREE WATCHER

by Christopher P. S...

I Dreamed

a Reindeer

T. D. Ashcraft
BUMP the
MONSTER

BUMP & the
NEW PET

DR.
ULYSSES
J.
PICKLEBOTTOM'S
GUIDE
TO
EVERYDAY
HOUSEHOLD
MONSTERS

AND HOW TO
DEFEAT THEM

by Christopher P. Stanley and Alex LeVasseur
Illustrations by Alex LeVasseur

T. D. Ashcraft
BUMP & the
FAMILY TREE

T. D. Ashcraft
BUMP & the
_ OF

I Dreamed I Was
a Turkey

I Dreamed

P. and Morgan L. Stanley

...ions by Tristan Seeger

www.JumpSplashBooks.com

Made in the USA
Monee, IL
06 June 2020